What's New?

By Jill Eggleton

Illustrated by Raymond McGrath

What's New?

Zed Zepperdee is an inventor. His job is to invent new and original products.

Sam and Toni are marketers. Their job is to persuade people to buy their products.

When Zed Zepperdee has completed his new product, Sam and Toni have a meeting. They discuss ways to launch the new product.

CLARIFY:

PROMOTE

A advertise

B illustrate

C sell

A, B, OR C?

. . . they're great!
Toni, this is Zepperdee's latest invention.
He really does come up with some zany stuff!
They should be easy to promote. Everyone is looking for a quick way to move around these days.
Yes, they're great. I can't wait to zip around in them myself.
Right! I'll do the advertisement for the paper and the billboard.
OK! I'll do a letter to Sharper Shoes and a flyer.
Marketing ideas for Electric shoes
shoe streakers

Advertisement

SHOE STREAKERS

THE WORLD'S FIRST ELECTRIC SHOES

Now Available

Get with it!
Get Shoe Streakers!
You will be AMAZED
at where you can go and how fast!

Smooth, effortless gliding
Solar powered

Hurry – limited stock!
Phone: Zepperdee Inventions 800-555-4786
Email: zepperdeeinventions@clone.mag

Billboard

QUESTION:

What words are used to persuade the reader to buy Shoe Streakers?

?

Letter

ZEPPERDEE INVENTIONS

May 4, 2004

Sharper Shoes
P.O. Box 27
7 Market Street
Ingle

Dear Sir/Madam,

We are pleased to announce the arrival of Shoe Streakers, the very latest in shoe technology. These amazing shoes are another innovative invention from Zed Zepperdee.

Shoe Streakers are electric shoes, powered by solar panels on the top of each shoe. The battery is concealed in the heel. These shoes are operated by a remote control. They have four small ballbearing wheels that provide a smooth and comfortable ride. The wheels are retractable, and the wearer can select indoor or outdoor just by the flick of a switch.

We have been testing the Shoe Streakers and have found that we can enjoy the world around us far more, as we don't need to concentrate on where to put our feet. Shoe Streakers are marvelous for young children who can't walk very fast. With a pair of Shoe Streakers, small children can keep up with adults. There is no need for clumsy strollers.

We have also found Shoe Streakers excellent for elderly people who are finding it difficult to walk. When they strap on a pair of Shoe Streakers, they can move effortlessly wherever they want to.

We are sure your customers will be impressed with these shoes. Shoe Streakers are available in all sizes and in a variety of styles and colors. If you wish to examine samples or want a demonstration of these incredible shoes, we can arrange this.

Yours faithfully,

Sam Hunt
Marketer

Zed Zepperdee Inventions
P.O. Box 54678
Bathworth

Flyer

SHOE STREAKERS

FREE TRIAL

Shoe Streakers

Zed Zepperdee has done it again – created another remarkable invention. These shoes are really electric!

We are offering a free trial of these amazing shoes on: Saturday, June 4
4 Temple Street, Bathworth

Bring the whole family for a fun time.
(Don't leave Granny behind. We have shoes for her, too!)

- Electric shoes are fun, safe, sensible, and can carry you anywhere, faster.
- Find out for yourself.
- We look forward to seeing you on Saturday.
- Phone 800-555-4786 to book your trial shoes.
- Visit our website – www.zepperdeeinventions.com

FACT OR OPINION?

A Fact is a statement that can be proved to be true.

An Opinion is a view or belief that is not based on fact or knowledge.

FACT	OPINION
Shoe Streakers are electric shoes	?
?	?

Sam and Toni's marketing of Shoe Streakers was a success.

Before long, people of all ages were zooming around on their Shoe Streakers. Elderly people thought they were cool because they could move again without their knees hurting. Parents thought they were cool because they didn't have to push strollers around. And kids thought they were really cool, even though they couldn't go as fast as scooters or skateboards.

But Zed Zepperdee was always inventing . . .

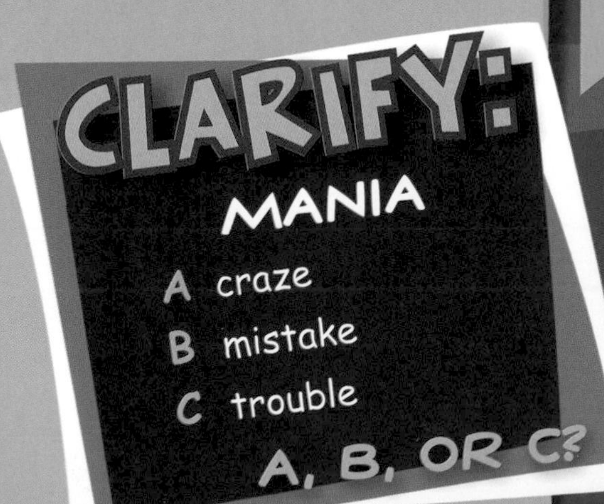

Yes, it feels odd to be in ordinary shoes now.
Zed has given us a new project.
What has he come up with this time?
. . . you'll love these
You'll love these. He has nvented two awesome hats. Let's get marketing.
Wow! These are original. They'll be easy to market.

Advertisements

- Now you can have your hands free.
- Rain-sensor device automatically unfolds umbrella.
- Simple push-button controls collapse.

Available in: Bright Fluorescent Colors, Spots, and Stripes

Be trendy on a rainy day!

Zepperdee INVENTIONS

Phone Zepperdee Inventions 800-555-4786
Email: zepperdeeinventions@clone.mag

Instant push-button flash

If there's an unforgettable moment – fumbling fingers can't undo the camera case!

Too late, it's gone!

But... not if you have a **FOTO HAT!**

Invest in a **FOTO HAT** now and capture the moment!

Phone Zepperdee Inventions 800-555-4786

Email: zepperdeeinventions@clone.mag

QUESTION:

What is meant by . . . **the ultimate in rainy weather protection?**

?

ANNOUNCING

TWO NEW ZEPPERDEE

UMBRELLA HAT AND FOTO

Look at these features:

- umbrella pops up in rain
- simple button
- concealed umbrella

FREE
Umbrella Hat

We are offering a free Umbrella Hat to the first 25 purchasers of a Foto Hat!

Umbrella Hat

Phone 800-555-4786 to secure these inventions now, or order on our website www.zepperdeeinventions.com

QUESTION:

What might persuade the reader to buy a Foto Hat?

?

INVENTIONS!

AT

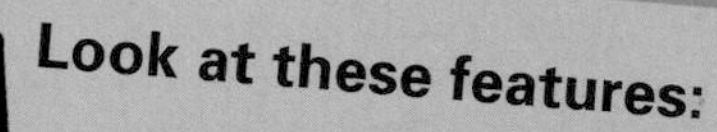

Look at these features:

- **instant photo at one touch**
- **automatic zoom**
- **concealed button**

. . . design a brochure

Zed Zepperdee had people calling up every day and asking for a brochure.

He told Sam and Toni they would have to design a brochure that showed all of his products.

PREDICT:

How do you think the brochure might look?

OK, let's draw up some ideas.
The front flap needs to grab attention!
We'll use color, interesting design, and pictures. If we don't grab attention first, they won't even open it up.
How about some of these ideas for the brochure?
Brochure ideas for Umbrella Hat and Foto Hat

Brochure

ZedZepperdee
INVENTIONS
The latest and greatest technology

The world's most amazing inventor

Zed Zepperdee products are . . . original, zany, fun, practical, wacky, funky, cool . . .
THE BEST!

PHONE 800-555-4786
www.zepperdeeinventions.com

SHOE STREAKERS

Zed Zepperdee has been inventing for several years but only recently has agreed to market some of his truly outstanding inventions. Now people throughout the world are enjoying ZZ products.

ZZ products

Electric Shoes

- Solar powered
- Remote control
- Inside/outside wheel options
- Smooth rolling
- Stylish
- Variety of colors and sizes

BRELLA HAT

include:

Umbrella Hat
- Rain sensor pop-up umbrella
- Easy push-button control for folding
- Range of bright fluorescent, colors, spots, and stripes
- All sizes

Foto Hat
- Lightweight
- Instant photo at one touch
- Automatic zoom, focus, and light control
- Six color choices
- Sizes small, medium, or large

DESCRIPTIVE WORDS:

Which words are adjectives?

Sensor Zany Funky
Bright Color
Smooth

Can you find more . . . ?

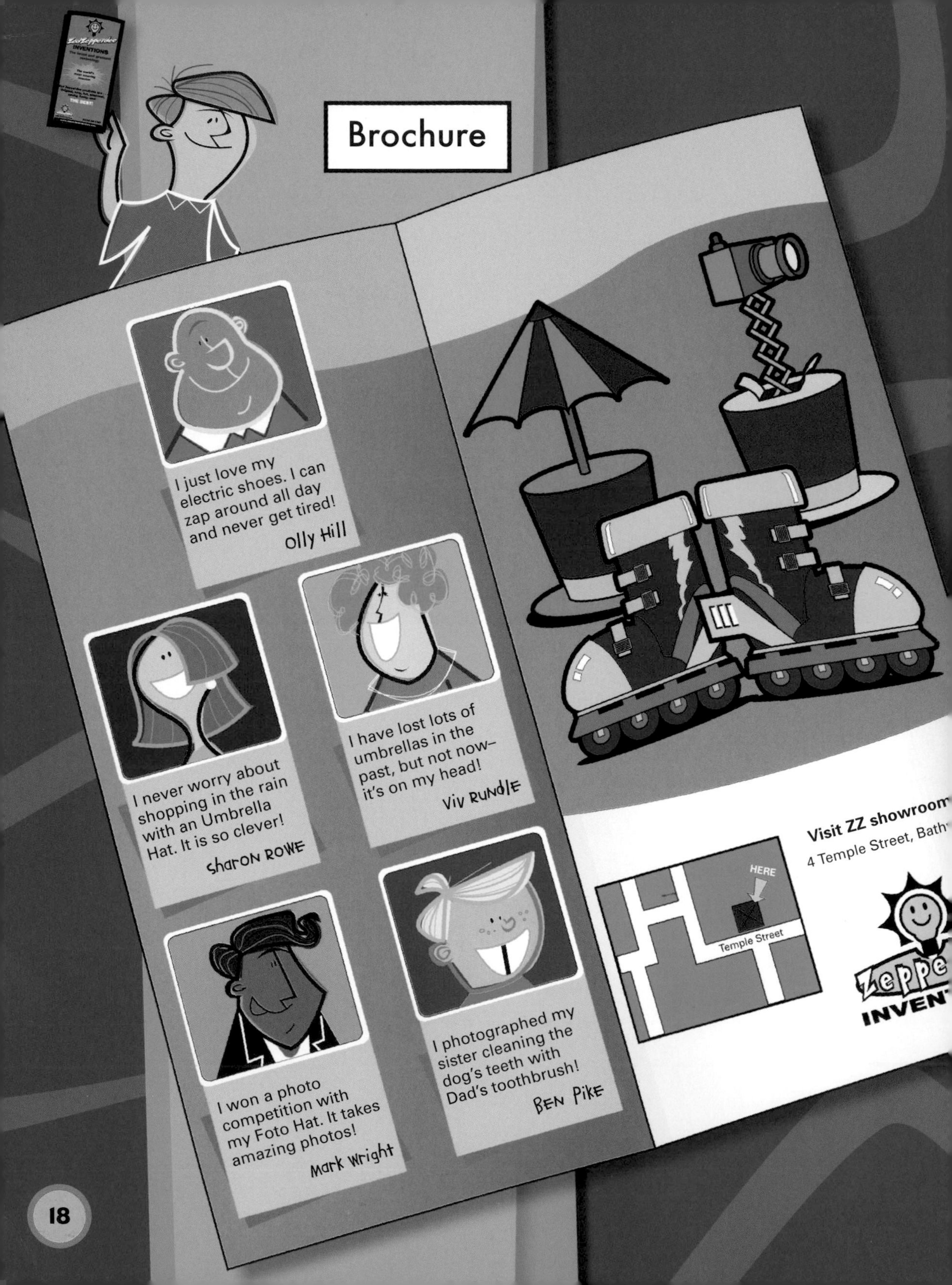

Brochure
I just love my electric shoes. I can zap around all day and never get tired!
Olly Hill
I never worry about shopping in the rain with an Umbrella Hat. It is so clever!
Sharon Rowe
I have lost lots of umbrellas in the past, but not now– it's on my head!
Viv Rundle
I won a photo competition with my Foto Hat. It takes amazing photos!
Mark Wright
I photographed my sister cleaning the dog's teeth with Dad's toothbrush!
Ben Pike
Visit ZZ showroom
4 Temple Street, Bath
HERE
Temple Street

QUESTION:

What might make the reader of this brochure want to visit a ZZ showroom?

?

Summary of Advertisement features

Emotive language	?
Instructions that involve the reader	? ? ?
Rhetorical questions	? ?
Personal pronouns to involve the reader	? ?
Repetitive text	? ?
Text that urges urgent action	? ?
Find some examples	?

Think about the Text

What connections can you make to advertisements and the effect they have on you?

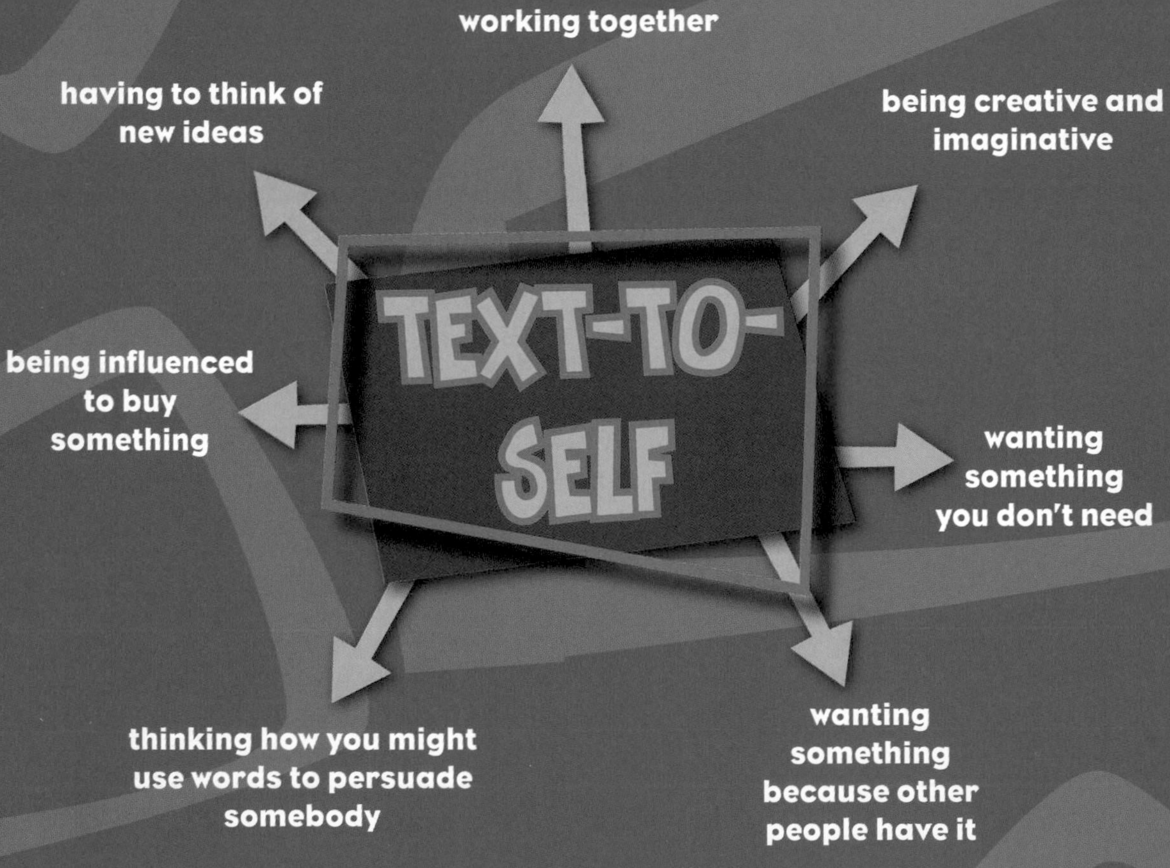

TEXT-TO-SELF

- working together
- having to think of new ideas
- being creative and imaginative
- being influenced to buy something
- wanting something you don't need
- thinking how you might use words to persuade somebody
- wanting something because other people have it

TEXT-TO-TEXT

Talk about other texts you may have read that have similar features. Compare the texts.

TEXT-TO-WORLD

Talk about situations in the world that might connect to elements in the text.

Planning an Advertisement

Choose a product or service to sell or learn about.

Think about the purpose of the advertisement.

- To invite further inquiries about the product or service
- To inform and excite interest in the product or service
- To give contact advice
- To influence the behavior and attitudes of people

Think about the audience the advertisement is targeting.

- Sports people
- Seniors
- Teenagers
- Car enthusiasts . . .

Think about the way you can use language to persuade the reader. You can use . . .

- Instructions that involve the reader personally
- Emotive language to excite the feelings of the reader
- Personal pronouns to involve the reader
- Text that urges urgent action
- Repetitive text so the message is remembered
- Rhetorical questions - questions that require no answers

Think about the way you can use images and design to gain the attention of the reader.

You can use graphics with impact, color, and eye-catching fonts ...

Advertisements can feature:

- Words used in an imaginative way – similes, metaphors, alliteration
- Attention-grabbing headlines
- Humor
- Promises
- Special offers to the reader
- Exaggeration
- Quotes from important people
- Abbreviations